For my family.

Thank you for always supporting my dreams –

however hair-brained they may seem...

Mary

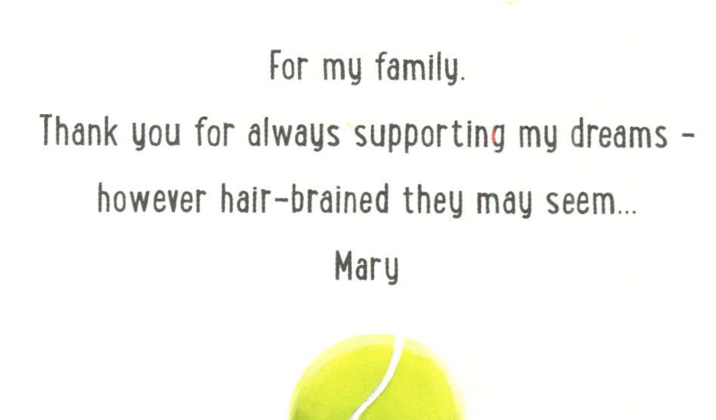

For Sofia,

a true Sports Star.

Anil

THIS BOOK BELONGS TO

Made with love by the team at

FIVE MILE

Fiona, Rocco, Graham, Kate, Mary & Julia

Five Mile,
the publishing division
of Regency Media
www.fivemile.com.au

First published in 2021 by Larrikin House

Printed in China 5 4 3 2 1

A catalogue record for this book is available from the National Library of Australia

I WANT TO BE A SPORTS STAR

MARY ANASTASIOU

ANIL TORTOP

My training day starts early
while dreaming in my bed.
Ribbons, medals, trophies;
all visions in my head.

I want to be a sports star
that no one else can beat.
Standing on a podium,
a strong and fit athlete.

1
3

I want to be a tennis star
and smash the Aussie Open.
A super athlete on the court,
my winning streak unbroken.

I want to be a swimmer,
the fastest in the pool.
Butterfly or Freestyle,
the Olympics I will rule.

I want to be a skater
and ride half pipes like a pro.
Grinding rails and hangin' Heelflips,
landing kick-flips on the go.

I want to be an athlete
running relay, distance, track.
To represent my country
and bring those medals back.

I want to be a footy star,
in stadiums packed out.
I'll leap for marks and kick big goals
that make the masses shout.

I want to be a surfer
and ride the cleanest waves.
I'll cut through EPIC barrels –
I'll be powerful and brave.

I want to ride in motocross,
leaving others in my dust.
Ripping 'round the muddy track,
my throttle at full thrust.

I want to be a gymnast
and backflip through the air.
With perfect poise, I'll point my toes
and grace the beams with flair.

I want to be a soccer star
like Ronaldo or Cahill.
I'll bend the ball like Beckham,
with style and natural skill.

I want to be a basketballer
slam dunking every hoop.
I'll shake the court with mighty jumps.
Now, watch me alley-oop!

I want to be a fencer –
all fears I'll disregard.
With silver Saber, suit and mask,
Allez. Assault. En-garde!

I want to be a cricket star
with my lucky wooden bat.
We'll win the mighty Ashes,
the crowd will roar 'HOWZAT!!'.

I've tried so many sports today
and learned so many skills.
I know I've brought my A-game
through all the thrills and spills.

1

ABOUT THE AUTHOR:

Author or the much loved *'I want to be...'* series, and the recently released *Jimmy Bottoms*, and *The Art of Making Friends* Mary Anastasiou is a self-confessed chocoholic, pluviophile and lover of all things Halloween - (especially vampires and ghosts).

When she's not writing books of her own, Mary uses her 35 years in design to create picture books for various Australian publishers.

With her heart firmly planted in kid lit, Mary writes books that she hopes will engage, inspire and empower little people on their journey to becoming big people.

ABOUT THE ILLUSTRATOR:

Anil Tortop was born and raised in Turkey. She moved to Australia in early 2011 and has been trying to get used to the local eight-legged house intruders and slithering visitors to her garden ever since. Anil also works as an animator and character/concept designer, but has been called away from this affair as her relationship with children's books becomes more serious. Nowadays, she lives with her husband in Brisbane, In their small home studio together, they call themselves "Children's Booksmiths."

COLLECT ALL THREE!

OTHER TITLES BY THIS AUTHOR: